Gracie's Gallery

A Magic Mirror Book

Written and Illustrated
by Kelly M. Houle

Hi, I'm George! I'm Gracie's older brother and the curator of Gracie's Gallery.

Gracie is four.

She likes to scribble. Every day she scribbles, and scribbles, and scribbles, but most people can't tell what her scribbles are supposed to be.

Like many artists, Gracie is misunderstood.

At first, I didn't understand Gracie's scribbling either. Her pictures didn't look like anything at all. Then, one day when I was standing in front of the refrigerator looking at all of Gracie's scribbles, I remembered something.

Whenever Gracie scribbles, she puts the shiny salt shaker on the edge of the paper.

"That's it!" I thought. When I put the salt shaker on one of Gracie's pictures, I couldn't believe my eyes!

The salt shaker was like a little mirror, and a perfect picture appeared in the reflection.

See for yourself.

Follow the directions above, on the inside cover of this book, to see what's so amazing about the scribbling of my younger sibling!

MOMMY GOING TO WORK

crayon on legal pad

Here the artist uses soft colors
to capture her subject.

DADDY WORKING ON THE COMPUTER

pencil and marker on envelope

Gracie often uses recycled materials
to create new work.

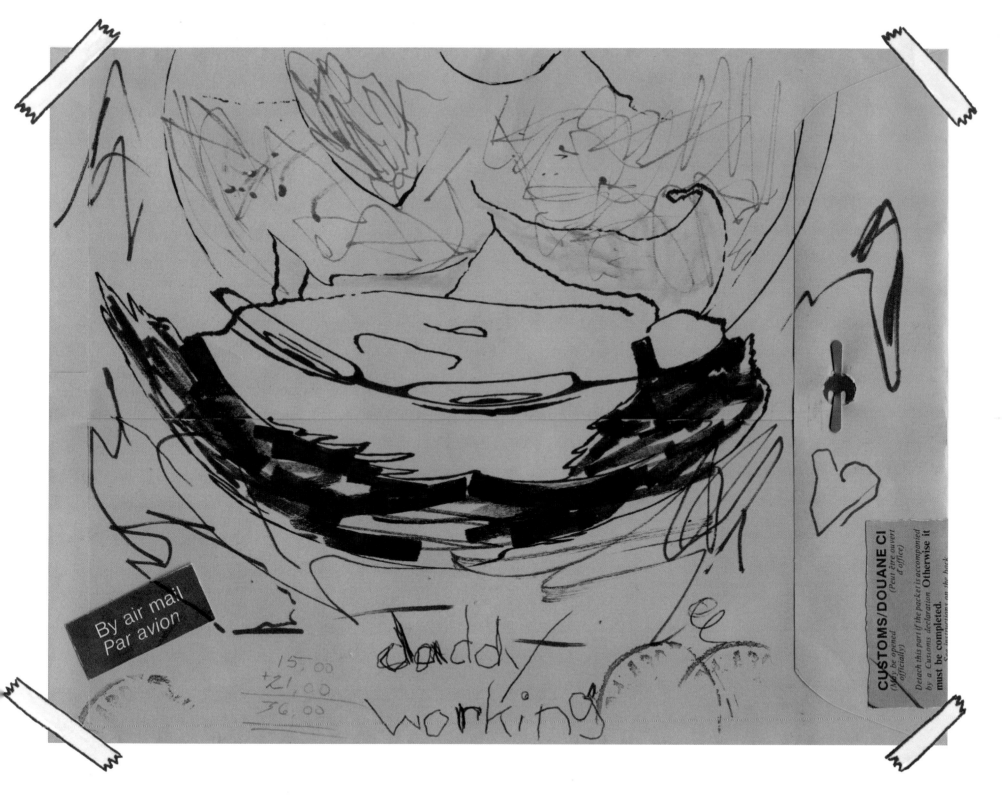

By air mail
Par avion

15,00
+21,00
36,00

daddy
working

GEORGE

crayon on green construction paper

I am honored to be one of Gracie's
first subjects. It looks just like me!

GUESS WHO

crayon and yarn on yellow construction paper

Here, Gracie follows in the footsteps of Rembrandt
in her choice of subject. This piece shows the
artist's first experimentation s with collage.

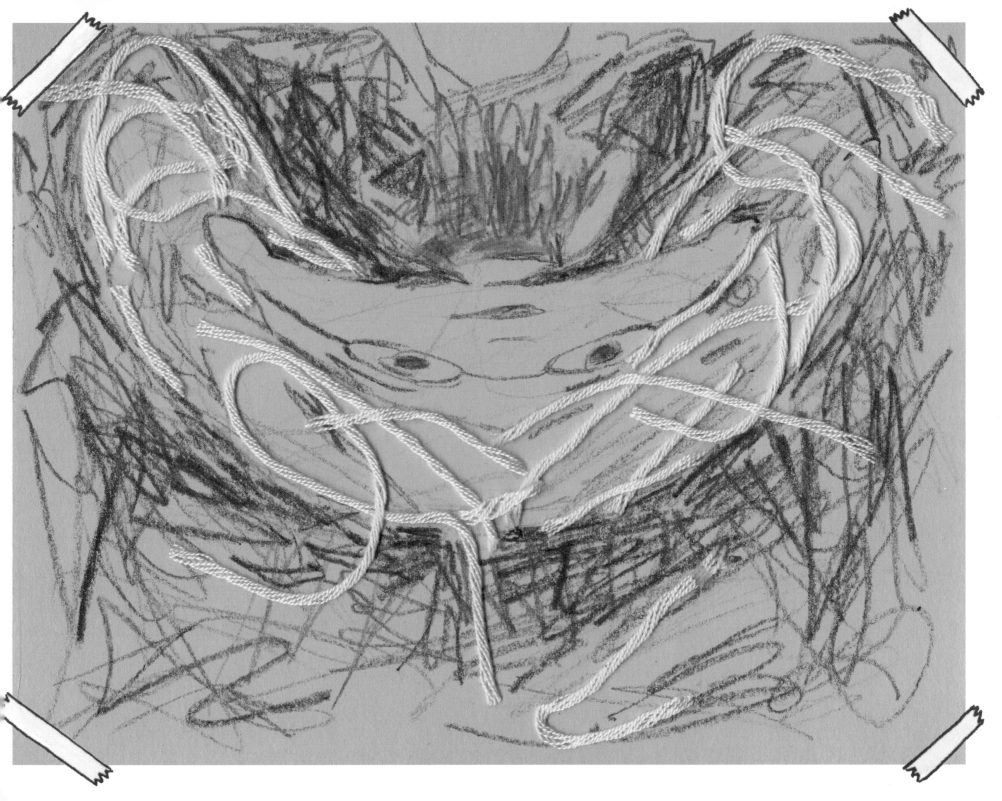

HENRY

crayon on blue construction paper

Notice the use of white crayon
to create a soft, furry texture.

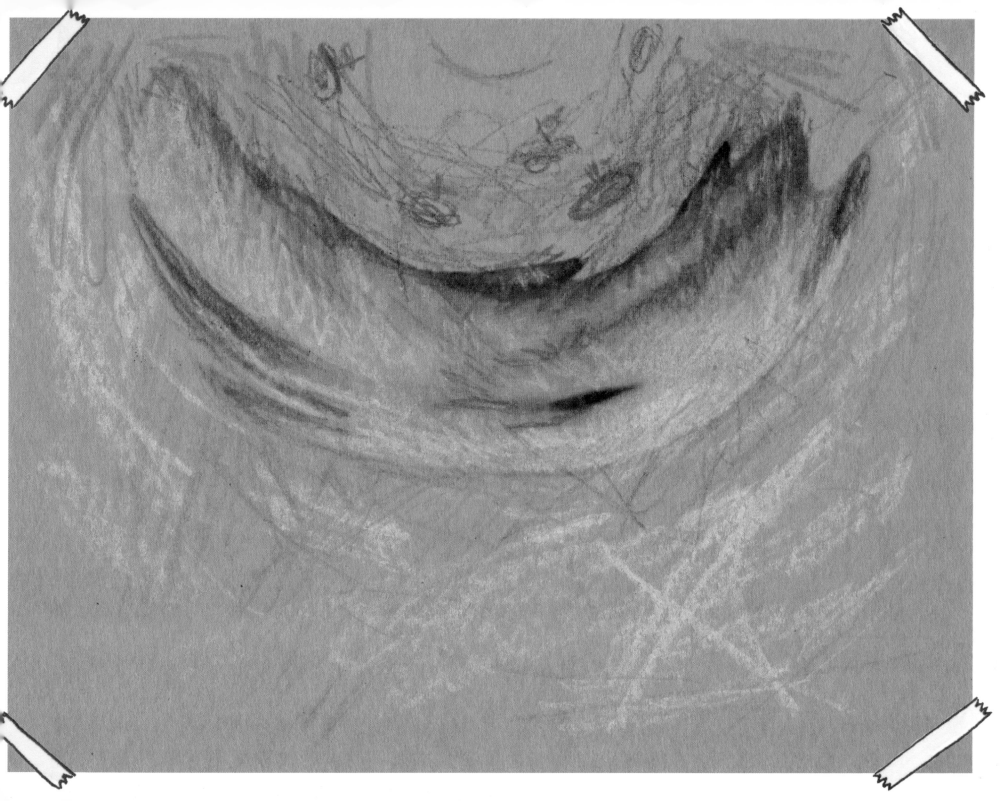

GEORGE AND HENRY'S TRICK

crayon on construction paper

This piece is a magical feat in itself!

MAXINE

crayon and glitter on paper

Here, the artist uses her favorite media to create a loving portrait of a dear family friend.

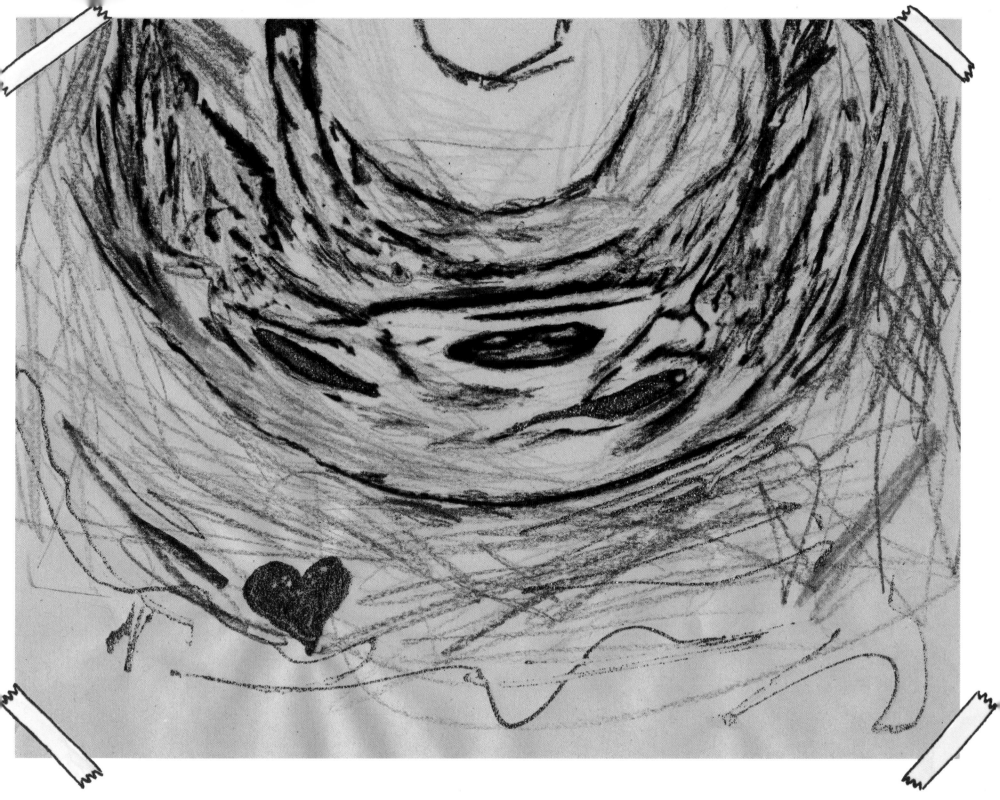

MAXINE'S FAVORITE TOYS

purple crayon on orange construction paper

Notice the artist's use of line to create form.

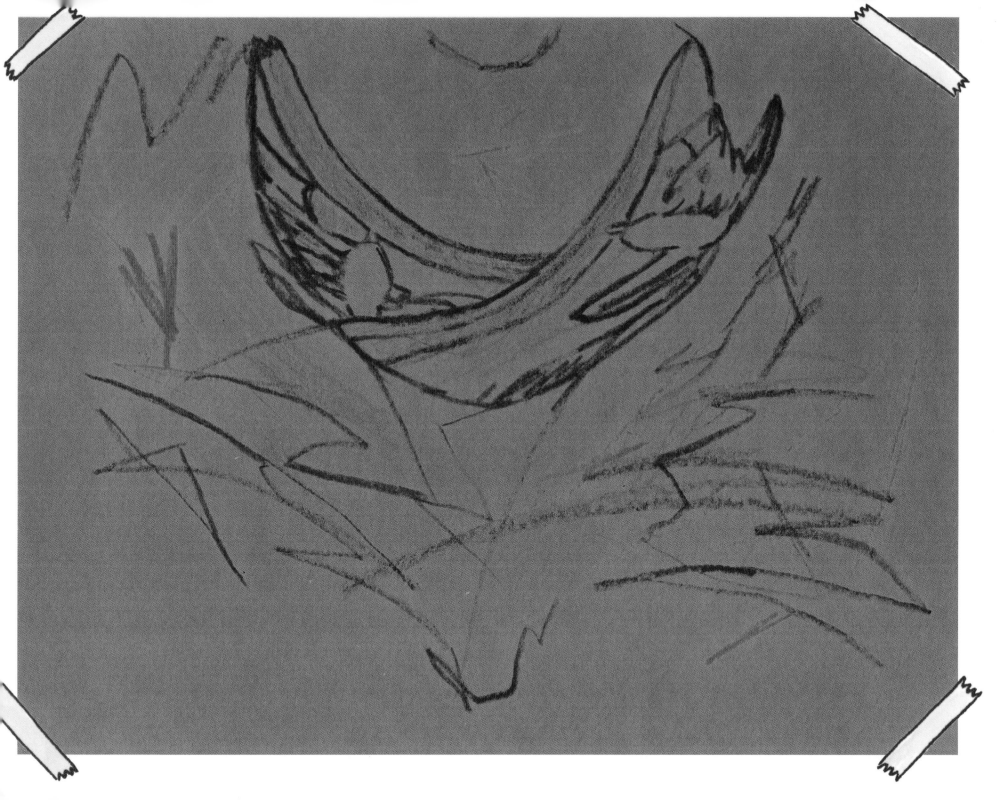

WHAT I FOUND IN THE YARD

crayon with twigs, leaves, and flowers

Here, Gracie uses natural materials
to camouflage her subject.

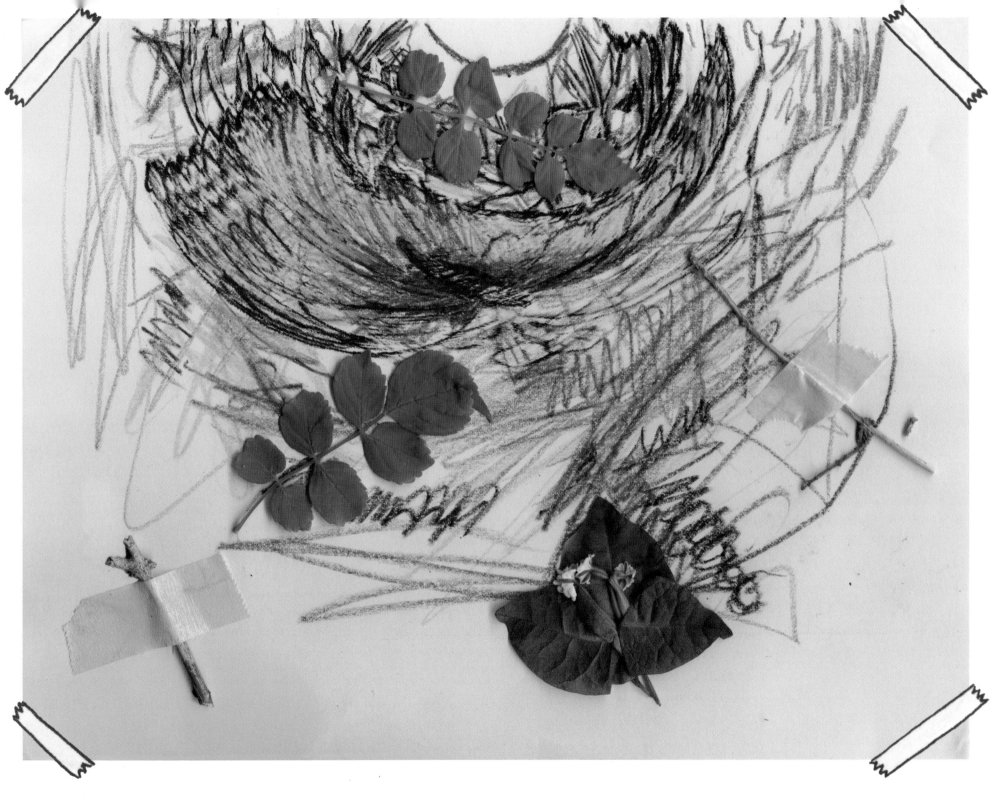

WHAT WE SAW AT THE ZOO

crayon on zoo map with feathers

A zoo map makes the perfect canvas
for Gracie's wildlife art.

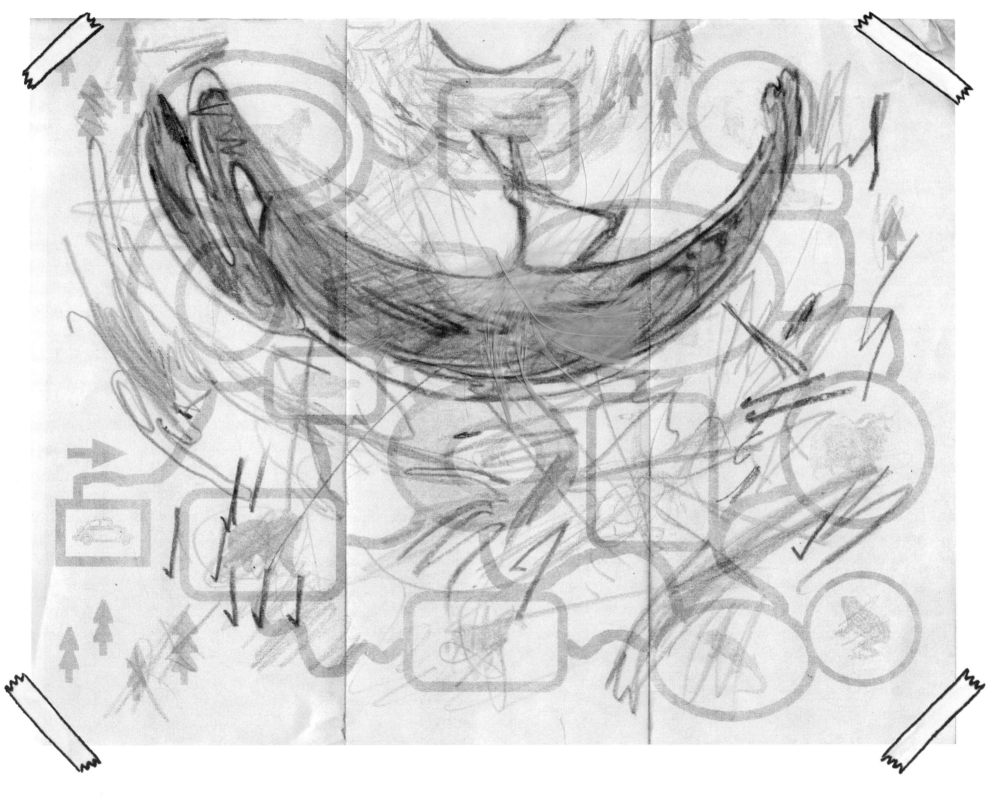

WHAT WE HAD FOR LUNCH

mixed media on back of restaurant menu

This piece provides a rare look into
the eating habits of a true artist.

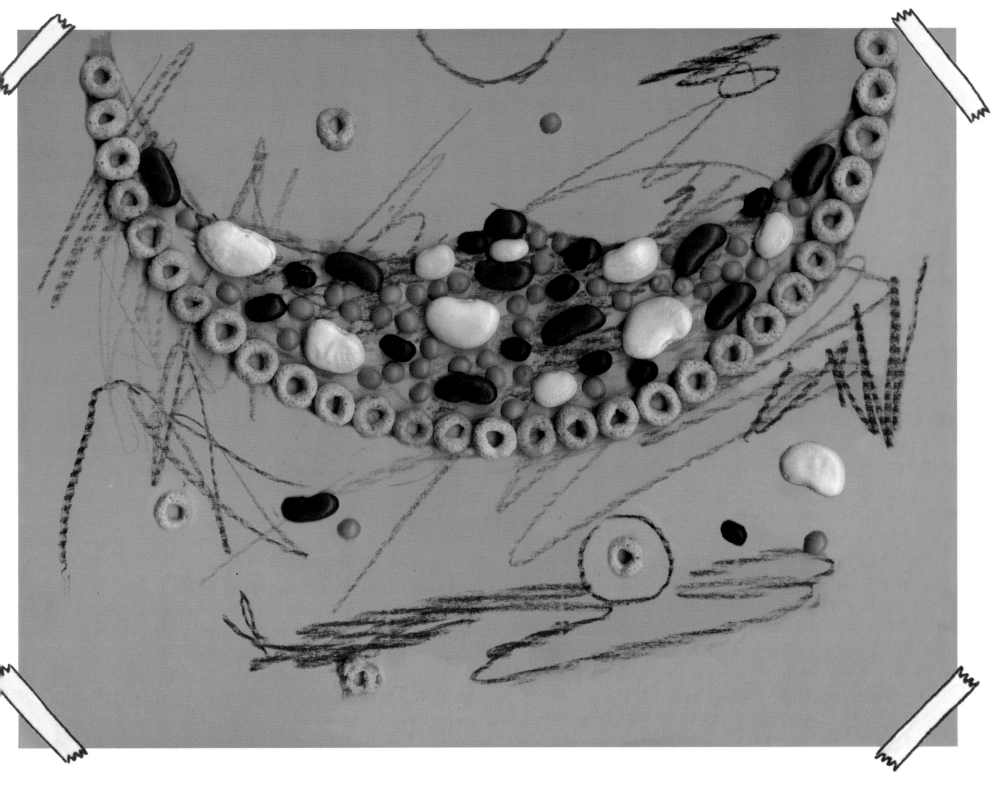

MY FAVORITE PLACE

paint and colored pencil on watercolor paper

This piece is a colorful impression
of the artist's residence.